Seriously Silly Stories

RUMPLY
CRUMPLY
STINKY
PIN

Compass Point Books
3109 West 50th Street, #115
Minneapolis, MN 55410

Visit Compass Point Books on the Internet at *www.compasspointbooks.com*
or e-mail your request to *custserv@compasspointbooks.com*

Library of Congress Cataloging-in-Publication Data
Anholt, Laurence.
  Rumply Crumply Stinky Pin / by Laurence Anholt. Illustrated by Arthur Robins.
    p. cm. — (Seriously silly stories)
Summary: In this version of the classic fairytale "Rumpelstiltskin," the miller's daughter
must guess her helper's name to keep her pet guinea pig.
ISBN 0-7565-0633-6 (hardcover)
  [1. Fairy tales. 2. Humorous stories.] I. Title II. Series: Anholt, Laurence. Seriously
silly stories.
  PZ8.A577Ru 2004
  [E]—dc22   2003017955

For more information on *Rumply Crumply Stinky Pin,* use
FactHound to track down Web sites related to this book.

1. Go to *www.compasspointbooks.com/facthound*
2. Type in this book ID: 0756506336
3. Click on the *Fetch It* button.

Your trusty FactHound will fetch the best Web sites for you!

About the Author
Laurence Anholt is one of the UK's leading authors. From his home in
Dorset, he has produced more than 80 books, which are published all
around the world. His Seriously Silly Stories have won numerous
awards, including the Smarties Gold Award for "Snow White and the
Seven Aliens."

About the Illustrator
Arthur Robins has illustrated more than 50 picture books, all of them
highly successful and popular titles, and is the illustrator for all the
Seriously Silly Stories. His energetic and fun-filled drawings have been
featured in countless magazines, advertisements, and animations. He
lives with his wife and two daughters in Surrey, England.

First published in Great Britain by Orchard Books, 96 Leonard Street, London EC2A 4XD

Text © Laurence Anholt 1996/Illustrations © Arthur Robins 1996

Seriously Silly Stories

RUMPLY
CRUMPLY
STINKY
PIN

Written by Laurence Anholt
Illustrated by Arthur Robins

 COMPASS POINT BOOKS

Minneapolis, Minnesota

There was once a country where everyone had silly names.

They were called Mrs. Mouse Dropping or Roland Camelbelly, and they called their children Little Custardlump or Teeny-Tiny Toenail Clipping.

But the person with the silliest name of all was the king himself, and he was very proud of it.

His full title was His Royal Niceness Marvin Eggbeard Pajamadance Birdwhistle Gormangeek Bob-a-job Kneepickle Burp Glub-glub Globba Blobin Eeeeee Woomph Paint-Your-Mother-Green—Junior III, which is a pretty good name for a king.

His Royal Niceness
Marvin Eggbeard
Pajama

Now, in this country lived a miller by the name of Eyebrow Snailsocks. Eyebrow had a beautiful daughter who he was always bragging about. "Not only is she beautiful," he would say, "but she is clever, too."

"My daughter can do anything! Why, I bet she could... I bet she could... make string vests out of spaghetti!"

"Don't be silly, Daddy," the girl would say.

And everyone who knew old Eyebrow only laughed.

But one day, the king (whose name I have mentioned) heard of Eyebrow's idle boasts.

"Send your daughter to me," he ordered, "let's see how clever she really is."

The miller was very frightened, and his daughter began to shake and weep into her apron, but the king's order had to be obeyed.

Before she left, Eyebrow promised to buy his daughter anything she wanted to make up for the trouble his bragging had caused.

His daughter couldn't think of anything
offhand except perhaps a little fluffy guinea
pig for a pet. And this Eyebrow promised
her as soon as she returned from the palace.
(Assuming she was still wearing her head.)

And so it was that the young girl stood shaking before the king.

"Do you know who I am?" he demanded in a deep royal voice.

"Yes sir," whispered the girl. "You are His Royal Niceness Marvin Eggbeard Pajamadance Birdwhistle Gormangeek Bob-a-job Kneepickle Burp Glub-glub Globba Blobin Eeeeee Woomph Paint-Your-Mother-Green—Junior III."

"Exactly," said the king. "Now, your father has been boasting that you can knit string vests out of spaghetti. I have decided to lock you in a room full of spaghetti, and if it isn't all knitted into string vests by sunrise, I will personally tickle your armpits with a wet toothbrush."

Saying this, the king swept out of the room and went off to practice signing his name.

The miller's daughter was in despair. She looked at the mountain of spaghetti and thought of the little fluffy guinea pig she would never see. Then she wept into her apron again.

All of a sudden she heard a funny little laugh:

Tee hee hee hee !

And looking down at her feet she saw the strangest little man she had ever seen. He wore a pointy hat and had an orange beard, which was so long that he had wrapped it three times around his waist.

"I know," she sobbed. "I have to knit all this spaghetti into string vests. Otherwise, the king will tickle my armpits with a wet toothbrush."

"Oh please help me," sobbed the girl.

The little fellow grabbed an armful of spaghetti and pulled two enormous knitting needles from his pocket. But suddenly, he paused, and looked up at the girl.

The poor girl searched her apron pocket, which was soaked with tears, and finally pulled out a soggy toffee, which the little man seized with delight.

The girl danced with joy as vest after vest flew from the flashing needles.

Early in the morning the king brought
the miller to watch the toothbrush tickling.

Of course, he couldn't believe his eyes when he unlocked the door and saw that every last bit of spaghetti had been made into perfect little string vests, all with tomato buttons down the front, as neat as you please.

"What did I tell you?" boasted Eyebrow Snailsocks (pretending not to be surprised). "I said she was clever. My daughter can do anything! Why, I bet… I bet she could make dollar bills out of old fish."

"Oh Daddy!" groaned the miller's daughter. But it was too late. The king was already ordering a room to be filled to the ceiling with old fish.

"All right!" he shouted. "If she fails I'll...
let's see... I'll plant melon seeds between
her toes and... if she succeeds then... I'll
marry her."

Well, the miller's daughter didn't much
like the idea of having melon seeds planted
between her toes...

...but, on the other hand, she didn't like the idea of being married to the king either, especially if she was going to be called Her Royal Niceness Marvin Eggbeard Pajamadance Birdwhistle Gormangeek Bob-a-job, etc, etc.

As soon as she was alone with the mountain of fish she began to weep into her apron. Surely no one could make dollar bills out of old fish? Now she was sure she would never have the fluffy guinea pig her father had promised her.

Suddenly the room was filled with strange laughter...

Tee hee hee hee!

…and the little man stood before her
again, singing in his squeaky voice.

The girl told the little man about her father's bragging and the king's order that she should make dollar bills out of old fish.

She was just getting to the bit about the melon seeds, when the little man pulled a printing press from his pocket and began throwing the fish in one end and pulling crisp new dollar bills from the other, singing as he worked…

"Anything, anything," promised the poor girl, frantically searching her apron pockets. But alas! There was nothing there.

The girl gladly agreed and by sunrise not one minnow remained. The room was stacked to the ceiling with neatly folded, slightly smelly dollar bills.

"Let's marry immediately!" shouted the king throwing open the door.

Eyebrow jumped up and down with delight. "You see!" he yelled, "I told you she was clever. This girl can do anything! Why I bet… I bet…"

But the miller's daughter was gone,
down the stairs and out of the palace.

Later, as he walked home, the miller began to feel very sorry about all the fat lies he had been telling, and all the trouble he had caused.

So remembering his promise, he stopped
at the pet shop and bought his daughter the
cutest, fluffiest little guinea pig he could find.

The girl was delighted and soon forgot about the horrid king and the strange little man. But that night as she lay in her bed listening to her new pet running round and round on his squeaky wheel, she heard someone laughing outside her door . . .

45

The girl didn't wear her apron in bed, so she wept into her pajamas instead. "Don't take my guinea pig," she pleaded.

The little man felt sorry for her and said . . .

Okay kid.
we'll play a game.
I'll give you two days
to guess my name.

In a flash, he was gone. The girl lay
awake for the rest of the night thinking of
possible names for him.

The next evening, the little man returned.

Miller's daughter,
I must confess,
If I gave you forever,
you still wouldn't guess.

But the daring girl was determined to try. "Is it Scrambled Egg Foot?" she asked.

But the little man only laughed...

...and stroked his long orange beard.

"Is it Plum-Plum-Lemon-Moose Carpet Ears?" she asked hopefully.

The little man laughed even more.

"Well then, perhaps it's Hubert Crumpet Trumpet-Bottom?" the miller's daughter asked desperately.

The little man screeched with laughter and in a flash, he was gone, leaving the poor girl more miserable than ever.

The old miller didn't like to see his daughter unhappy, so at breakfast he told her a story to cheer her up.

"I was delivering flour yesterday when I saw the funniest thing; there was a little man wearing a string vest made of spaghetti, dancing outside a tiny caravan, and he was singing the most peculiar song."

"Can you remember the song?" asked the girl, her eyes lighting up.

"Well, yes," said her father. He cleared his throat and sang:

> I sing and dance a little jig,
> Soon I'll have that guinea pig.
> They can weep a bowl of tears.
> They won't guess my name
> in a billion years.

"It did make me laugh I can tell you!"

"Yes, yes, but didn't he mention his name?" shouted the girl.

"Whose name, my dear?" asked the puzzled miller.

"The little man, you old toad!" snapped the girl.

"Oh no," said the miller, "he didn't."

The poor girl began to despair and a big tear ran down her pale cheek and into her boiled egg.

"Don't cry," said her father, "I can tell you his name—it was painted on the side of his caravan: Rumply Crumply Stinky Pin. Magician. (Spaghetti Vests A Speciality)."

"That's it," cried the girl clapping her hands with joy.

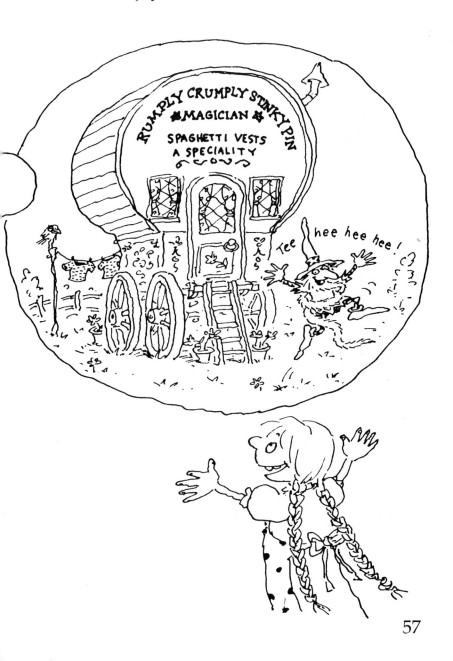

That night, as she was feeding her guinea pig, the little man appeared again.

"I'll just try again," said the clever girl. "I might be lucky this time. Is it Benny Badger-Brain or Eddy Earwax-Eater?"

The little man rolled with laughter.

"Perhaps it's Trevor Telephone Bone Helicopter-Head!"

The little man was lying on the bed, kicking his legs in the air.

"I'll give it one last try," said the miller's daughter, "and the guinea pig is yours. Is it... Rumply Crumply Stinky Pin?"

The little man almost choked with rage and vanished in a clap of thunder, filling the air with a strange smell of burning spaghetti and old fish.

So, the miller's daughter lived happily ever after with her guinea pig and her old father, who hardly ever told lies anymore.

"What will you call your little pet?"
asked Eyebrow Snailsocks one day. "How
about Guinea-Winnie-Winkie-Wigs or
Pinkie-Poky-Porky-Piggy Pants?"

"Oh no, Daddy," said the girl. "I think I'll just call him… Fred."

"That is a very silly name," said Eyebrow Snailsocks.

And it was.

Moral: A guinea pig is for life, not just for Christmas.